LOST!

A Dog Called Bear

RAINBOW
STREET
SHELTER

LOST!

A Dog Called Bear

by Wendy Orr

illustrations by Susan Boase

Henry Holt and Company ❖ New York

Henry Holt and Company, LLC
Publishers since 1866
175 Fifth Avenue
New York, NY 10010
mackids.com

Henry Holt® is a registered trademark of Henry Holt and Company, LLC.
Text copyright © 2011 by Wendy Orr
Illustrations copyright © 2011 by Susan Boase
All rights reserved.

Library of Congress Cataloging-in-Publication Data
Orr, Wendy.
Lost! A dog called Bear / Wendy Orr ; illustrations by Susan Boase.—1st ed.
p.   cm.—(Rainbow Street Shelter ; 1)
Summary: When Logan's dog runs away as he and his mother are moving to
a new home after his parents separate, a girl named Hannah,
who longs for a dog of her own, finds him.
[1. Dogs—Fiction.   2. Lost and found possessions—Fiction.   3. Divorce—
Fiction.   4. Moving, Household—Fiction.]   I. Boase, Susan, ill.   II. Title.
PZ7.O746Lo 2011   [Fic]—dc22   2010029886

ISBN 978-0-8050-8931-8 (HC)
1 3 5 7 9 10 8 6 4 2

ISBN 978-0-8050-9381-0 (PB)
1 3 5 7 9 10 8 6 4 2

First Edition—2011 / Book designed by April Ward
Printed in June 2011 in the United States of America by
R. R. Donnelley & Sons Company in Crawfordsville, Indiana

For Bear, and for all the other
dogs, from Puppy to Harry, who
have come into my life

—W. O.

1

What Bear liked, almost more than anything else in the world, was riding in the
back of the pickup truck. He liked racing
from side to side to see everything going
past, sniffing the wind as it flapped his
jowls and ruffled his fur, and barking at
dogs on the ground.

The other thing Bear liked almost more than anything else in the world was bossing sheep and making them go where he wanted.

But what he liked best of all, more than anything else in the world, was Logan—because Logan was his boy.

What Logan liked, almost more than anything else in the world, was riding around the farm in the back of the pickup truck. He liked bouncing over the bumps, singing into the wind as it ruffled his hair, and watching Bear race from side to side. He liked the way his friends from town thought riding in the back with him was as cool as all the things he thought would be cool in town.

The other thing Logan liked, almost more than anything else in the world, was walking around the farm with his dad and watching Bear herd the sheep wherever they were supposed to go.

What he liked best of all, more than anything else in the world, was Bear—because Bear was his dog.

But now Logan's mother and father had sold the farm. His dad and Bear were going to work on a big ranch in the mountains, and Logan and his mom were moving to the city.

Logan felt like the turkey's wishbone being pulled apart after Thanksgiving dinner. What he wished was for everything to be the same way it always had been.

"Your dad and I are still friends," said his mom. "We just can't live together anymore."

"It doesn't change how I feel about you," said his dad. "I still love you as much as ever."

"But what about Bear?" asked Logan. "How's he supposed to understand?"

"He'll like it on the ranch," said his dad. "They've got a couple of working dogs already. Bear will get along fine with them."

"He'll hate it!" shouted Logan. "He'll miss me—he needs to come with me!"

His dad didn't tell him off for shouting. He pulled Logan close and hugged him. "Not as much as I'll miss you," he said. "But maybe you're right. Maybe Bear should go with you."

"The yard in our new house is very small," said Logan's mom.

"I'll walk him every day," said Logan. "Bear will be all right, as long as he is with me."

What Hannah liked, almost more than anything else in the world, was going to the beach. She liked splashing through the waves with her friends and running on the sand, feeling the wind flip her ponytail as if it was as happy as she was.

But what Hannah liked more than anything was dogs—and what she wanted, more than absolutely anything else in the world, was a dog of her own.

"Our yard's not big enough," said her mom.

"I'd walk it every day," said Hannah.

"Dogs stink!" said her dad.

"I'd give it a bath," said Hannah.

"You'll forget to feed it," said her mom.

"I'd never forget," said Hannah.

2

The moving van came early in the morning. The moving men packed up all the boxes and furniture that Logan and his mom were taking to their new house. They left behind the boxes and furniture that Logan's dad was taking to his new home.

Logan hugged his dad as tight as he

could so that he'd have to get in the car with them, and his dad hugged him back so tight that Logan felt like a quivery jelly inside. But his dad still said good-bye.

Then Logan and Bear got into the back seat of the station wagon, his mom got into the driver's seat, and they drove away. Bear stuck his head out the window and barked. Logan stuck his head out the other window and waved good-bye until he couldn't see his house or his dad anymore.

It was a hot, dry day, and the dust from the driveway drifted in the windows and made his mom sneeze.

"Roll up your window," she said. "I'll turn on the air conditioner."

"I like the dust!" said Logan.

He rolled the window up, but he left a good wide crack at the top to let a little more of the farm's dirt blow in and go with them to the city.

Logan had been to the city before, but it had never been as far as it was today. The car had never been so hot, and Bear had never raced back and forth across the back seat so much. He stood on Logan's bare legs with his sharp nails.

"Ouch, Bear!" shouted Logan.

Bear leaned against him and drooled down Logan's neck.

"Yuck, Bear!" shouted Logan.

Bear licked Logan's legs, and Logan shoved him away. It wasn't nearly as much fun riding in the car with Bear as it was in the back of the pickup. "Maybe you should have gone with Dad, Bear," he snapped.

On the way to her friend Amy's house, Hannah passed a sign that said RAINBOW STREET ANIMAL SHELTER, with an arrow pointing up a narrow street.

"Could we go there?" Hannah asked her mom every time they passed the sign.

"It would just make you sad," said her mom. "And you would want to bring home a dog."

"I already want to bring home a dog," said Hannah. "And I wouldn't be sad if I could."

But her mom always sighed, "Oh, Hannah!" and drove on past.

At lunchtime, Logan and his mom stopped at Terri's Take Out. It was across the road from a wide white beach with rolling, crashing blue surf. Dogs weren't allowed on this beach, so his mom parked in the shade, and Logan walked Bear around the parking lot.

Then they put Bear back in the car and rolled the window down so he could sniff the fresh air, and they went into Terri's

Take Out for lunch. Logan looked out at
the ocean and for the first time since he'd
learned they were moving, a sparkle of
hope flickered through his black thoughts.

"Are we going to live near the beach?" he asked, as they walked back to the car.

"Pretty close," said his mom. "Too far to walk, but a short drive."

"Could I ride my bike?"

"When you're older," said his mom.

Logan's sparkle of hope fizzled and died. He didn't want to be older in their new house. He didn't want to have a birthday without his dad. He wanted to pretend they were just going to the beach for this last weekend of summer vacation and would be back in their old home when school started again.

His eyes blurred as he got into the car, and he squeezed them so tight shut that no tears could sneak through. His mom pulled back onto the highway toward their new home.

"How long till we get there?" he asked.

"About an hour," said his mom.

Logan opened his eyes and wiggled back in his seat. He reached over for Bear—and suddenly the hot day turned cold. He felt as if he'd been dunked in a giant bucket of ice.

"Mom," he said, in a sharp, tight voice, "where's Bear?"

3

Bear was not in the Terri's Take Out parking lot. Logan and his mom raced all around it, shouting Bear's name and looking everywhere a dog could possibly hide. They asked everyone in the restaurant and the playground and the gas station next door.

No one had seen a lost dog.

"Maybe he went to the beach," said Logan.

"He couldn't have crossed the highway," his mom said. "It's too busy. It's more likely he tried to follow us when we left."

She drove slowly down the road to where Logan had realized Bear was gone. Cars honked behind them, but Logan and his mom didn't care. All they cared about was finding Bear.

There was no lost dog running along the side of the highway.

"He might have tried to head for home," said his mom and turned the car around again, creeping back toward the farm until they knew they'd gone farther than Bear could have possibly run.

There was no lost dog heading toward his old home.

"We'll check the beach just in case," said Logan's mom and turned around again.

They parked right across from Terri's Take Out and ran down a path to the beach.

"Bear!" shouted Logan.

"Here, Bear!" shouted his mom.

Their voices were small against the noise of the water and the people shouting and playing. There were surfers carrying surfboards to the water or struggling out of their wetsuits; there were families setting up beach umbrellas or having picnics; there were little kids splashing in the shallows or building sand castles, kids on boogie boards or playing Frisbee, grandparents walking or taking pictures.

"BEAR!" roared Logan, like a desperate lion.

The people nearby turned to stare.

"Not a real bear," explained Logan's mom. "A dog named Bear."

"Because he looked like a bear cub when he was a puppy," said Logan. "But now he's lost. Here, Bear!"

They ran from one group of people to the next, asking if anyone had seen a shaggy black Border collie, with a white neck, three white paws, and one floppy white ear.

No one had.

"It's no good, Logan," said his mom. "I should have known he couldn't have crossed that road."

Logan followed his mom back up the beach. His stomach was swirling sickly, but however bad he felt, he knew Bear would feel worse.

Three boys jogged past. "Have you seen a lost dog?" Logan called.

"A big black-and-white dog?"

Logan felt as if he was choking. He nodded.

"He was running that way!"

 "About twenty minutes ago!"

Suddenly Logan could breathe again. "Thanks!" he shouted.

Logan and his mom raced back the way they'd come, kicking through the soft white sand. They stopped at the path to the highway, doubled over to catch their breath.

There was no black-and-white dog.

They began to run again. *We've got to see him soon!* Logan thought, and shouted again. "Here, Bear!"

They ran on the hard wet sand where the sea had just gone out, and swerved up to ask a family spreading their towels on the high dry sand.

"Have you seen a lost dog?"

"Sorry," said the dad. "We just got here."

Logan and his mom ran on. Their faces were red, their T-shirts were wet with sweat, and their chests were hurting.

They asked two girls reading on the sand.

The girls hadn't seen a dog all morning.

Neither had a boy wading in from the surf with his board.

But a mom tidying up a picnic said, "He was here about fifteen minutes ago."

"I gave him part of my hot dog," said her little boy.

"He went that way," said the mom. She pointed back the way Logan and his mom had come.

4

That morning, Hannah had woken up with such a wonderful idea that her ponytail quivered.

If her parents didn't have time to help take care of a dog, there might be other people who already had a dog and didn't have time to take care of it. They might need someone to take their dog for walks and play with it.

She got out paper and markers. She printed HANNAH THE DOG WALKER on the top. She drew paw prints underneath and her phone number at the bottom.

"You can't do that!" her mom exclaimed. "It's not safe to put your phone number up on posters everywhere."

"I could take it to the Rainbow Street Animal Shelter," said Hannah. "They could give it to people who want a dog but don't have enough time to take it for walks."

"Hannah!" sighed her mother. "You are not going to the animal shelter. I don't want to talk about it anymore."

Logan and his mom ran up and down the beach for three hours. They stopped for a drink twice, but the rest of the time they ran—and asked if anyone had seen a lost black-and-white dog.

"Ten minutes ago," said someone.

"He was just here," said someone else.

"Half an hour ago," said a third.

They all pointed in different directions.

A girl rubbing on sunscreen pointed to the path above the beach.

A mother pushing a child on a swing pointed back to the beach.

A man packing up his sailboat pointed back to the first beach.

This way and that way and back again, Logan and his mom ran, kicking through sand, pushing through people, calling and looking. It was like a nightmare that they couldn't wake out of.

Finally it was so late that the beach was not crowded anymore, and they knew that if Bear was anywhere around, they'd be able to see him, and he would see them.

"I'm sorry, Logan," said his mom. "We have to go on to the house. I'll figure out what to do when we get there."

"They must have all seen some other dog," said Logan. "A dog who liked the beach."

He felt as if an invisible monster had chewed a ragged black hole inside him where his happiness used to live. All the time they'd been running up and down the beach, poor Bear had been lost and frightened somewhere else—and now they might never find him.

But worst of all was wishing he'd never pushed Bear away and told him he should have gone with Dad after all.

Hannah had been in a grumpy mood all day, ever since her mother had said she couldn't go to the animal shelter. Her ponytail moped around her neck, and she couldn't think of anything she wanted to do.

Suddenly, the grumpiness dissolved like a Popsicle on the sidewalk.

Her dad was coming home from work. He was driving into the driveway and parking in the carport like he always did. There was just one thing different.

In the back of his pickup truck was a dog.

5

The dog was black and furry, with a white neck, three white paws, and one floppy white ear.

"What on earth is that dog doing there?" Hannah's mom demanded.

"How did that dog get there?" her dad echoed.

"Hannah!" they shouted together. "Get down from there!"

But Hannah was already sitting in the back of the truck with her arms around the dog. The dog was licking her face. His tongue was warm, wet, and tickly, and he was panting fast as if he was excited.

Hannah was excited too. If she'd been a balloon she'd have been ready to burst.

She jumped down from the truck and threw her arms around her father. "Thank you, thank you, thank you!" she squealed.

"But, Hannah," her dad began.

"We can't keep it," said her mom.

Hannah didn't hear. She ran inside to get a bowl of water for the thirsty dog. The dog jumped down after her, waiting at the front door till she came out. Hannah patted him while he drank big splashing gulps with his long red tongue.

"He's so soft," she told her parents. "And so nice and friendly. I'm going to call him Surprise, because he was the biggest surprise I ever got."

"Me too," said her dad.

"You can't call him anything," said her mom. "He's got to go back to where he came from."

"As soon as we can figure out where that is!" said her dad.

"Did you see any dogs where you were working today?" asked her mom.

"A few." Hannah's dad got out his cell phone. "He must have jumped into the wrong truck when we went home."

He phoned everyone he worked with, but the answer was always the same: no one had lost a dog. No one had even seen a stray dog.

Nobody wants him! thought Hannah. *Nobody except me!* She ran into the garage to find a piece of rope, and looped it through the ring on the dog's collar. There was a metal tag on the ring.

"Bear," Hannah read in a small voice. "And there's a phone number."

Her dad got out his cell phone again.

"The number's been disconnected. It's a good thing they put their last name on the tag, so we can try to find them."

"Imagine how worried they must be!" said her mom.

Hannah didn't want to imagine, but she did. She imagined them like Papa Bear, Mama Bear, and Baby Bear, except instead of porridge they'd be saying, "Who's been taking my dog?"

She didn't want to be Goldilocks.

"And imagine how happy they'll be when we give the dog back," said her dad. "We have to find them."

But when he phoned Information, there were no new phone numbers for Bears anywhere in the whole state.

"So we'll have to look after Surprise," said Hannah. "At least until we find the Bears."

Surprise pricked up his ears.

"He knows his new name already!" Hannah said. "He's a very smart dog."

She tugged the piece of rope. "Come on, Surprise!" and led him into the backyard.

Surprise followed happily.

"See how good he is!" Hannah told her parents. She went around to the front step for the bowl of water, shutting the gate behind her.

Surprise leapt over the fence and back onto the truck.

"No, Surprise!" Hannah whispered, and tried to push him into the yard again before her parents noticed.

It was too late.

"We can't keep him," said her mom. "He'll run away again, and this time he might get hurt."

6

Logan and his mom's new house was in the middle of a city. There were houses beside it, houses across the road, and houses behind it. The yard was small and the fence was tall.

All Logan cared about was that there was no dog. He looked in the yard, and he looked back down the road, because Bear was the smartest, fastest dog in the world, and Logan almost believed that he might have already found his way to their new home. But even Bear wasn't smart enough to find a house he'd never been to or fast enough to follow a car down the highway.

Inside, the house was jumbled full of furniture and boxes. The moving men had

put the beds in the bedroom and the couch in the living room, but Logan's bedroom was so crammed with boxes he had to scramble from one to another to get to the window. It could have been fun if he hadn't felt like crying.

Hannah had thought it was the best day of her life, and now it was the worst. She'd felt like a balloon ready to burst with happiness, and now her parents had pricked the balloon with a pin.

"We'll have to take him to the animal shelter," said her dad. "They can look after him properly while they find the people he belongs to."

"*I* can look after him properly!" Hannah wanted to shout, but she didn't because she'd seen him jump over the fence too.

Hannah sat on the ground with her arms around Surprise's neck for a long, long time. Finally she pushed away and looked into his bright brown eyes. "Don't worry. If we can't find your people, I'll look after you!"

Surprise licked her face, and they got into the back of the pickup.

"It might be easier if Dad went by himself," said her mom.

"I want to go," said Hannah. It was the biggest lie she'd ever told because she didn't want to go at all. She just couldn't let Surprise go without her.

Her dad tied the other end of the rope to a ring in his toolbox so Surprise had enough room to look around but not enough to jump out. Hannah gave him one more hug and got into the front of the truck between her parents.

When they turned at the sign for the Rainbow Street Animal Shelter, Hannah remembered how much she'd wanted to go there every single time they'd driven past. She'd never thought it would be the saddest day of her life.

Rainbow Street was short and narrow. At the end, surrounded by a tall wire fence, was a big garden with shady trees and green lawns. The building at its front was pale blue with a bright rainbow arching over the cheery, cherry red door.

Hannah knew that they had to leave Surprise here. She knew that he had to go back to the Bear family, and she knew she'd always be sad that she couldn't keep him. But this didn't look like a sad place, and for the first time, she felt the tiniest sliver of hope that something good could still happen.

The hope wasn't big enough to stop her eyes from being so blurry she could hardly see to untie Surprise's rope. It wasn't big enough to stop tears from splashing onto her cheeks as he jumped out of the truck and licked her face again. By the time they opened the gate and latched it behind them, that golden sliver of hope was so small it was nearly invisible.

But it was still there.

And so when Surprise heard all the other dogs barking and his happy wagging tail began to droop with nervousness, Hannah straightened up till her own ponytail bounced. Her voice came out stronger than she'd thought it would, like someone who'd hardly been crying at all.

"Come on, Surprise! It'll be all right."

7

"Can I help you?" It was an old man's voice, deep and gravelly.

Hannah stared in amazement because the only person she could see was a young woman with long dark hair wound up above a kind face and a name tag that said MONA.

"That's Gulliver," said Mona, pointing

to a gray parrot on a perch above the desk. "He likes being the receptionist."

"Gulliver!" repeated the parrot.

"We have found a lost dog," said Hannah's dad.

"Poor little guy," said Mona as she came around the other side of the desk to see Surprise. She squatted down beside him and felt him all over while Hannah's dad explained what had happened. A small brown stumpy-tailed dog followed her and sniffed Surprise as if she were checking too.

"The vet will have a look later, but he seems okay," Mona said. "I wonder if he's been microchipped."

She got an electronic wand from her desk and ran it over Surprise's neck and shoulders. There was no beep.

"That's a shame," Mona sighed. "Well,

let's hope the owners find us. He's such a lovely dog."

Surprise was panting nervously. Hannah squatted down beside him and put her arm around his neck. Surprise licked her as if he was saying thank you.

"Juan will take him now," Mona said as a gray-haired man came in.

"Hola, amigo!" said the parrot in his scratchy old-man's voice.

"Say good-bye, Hannah," said her mom.

But the gray-haired man smiled. "Maybe Hannah'd like to see where the dog's going to stay?"

His voice was the same as the parrot's.

Hannah nodded.

"Okay," Mona said, and so did Hannah's mom.

Hannah kept her hand on Surprise's shoulder as they followed Juan out to the hall. The stumpy-tailed dog trotted back behind the desk, and a white cat in the windowsill sat up to wash her paws and watch Surprise leave.

On the other side of the hall were doors that said EXAMINATION ROOM and SURGERY, and then rooms on both sides full of cages with a dog, cat, rabbit, skunk, or possum dozing in each one.

"That's the hospital for the sick animals," said Juan. "But this guy will go out here." He opened the back door.

There was a big aviary full of birds on one side; behind it was another big wire enclosure with a tree in the middle and three fat hollow logs scattered around. "For the wild animals getting ready to be set free again," said Juan.

Across from the aviary, separated by a path and a fence, was an enclosure where cats lazed in the sun in front of their own small shelters, and another for rabbits. Wooden walls separated them so the cats and bunnies didn't have to see each other, and neither of them had to see the dogs. On the lawn behind them, a three-legged goat was grazing. It looked quite happy, as if it hadn't noticed its hind leg was missing.

Juan opened a gate and they walked through to the dog area.

There was a dusty lawn in the middle, with two shade trees and a few bushes, with the kennels in a big U around it. Each kennel had its own fenced run; some had one dog; some had two. There were big dogs, short stubby-legged dogs, hairy dogs, and smooth dogs. Two in a run together were playing, some of the others were dozing, but most were watching Juan, Hannah, and Surprise.

They walked across the open area to an empty run.

Surprise's tail drooped, and so did his head. He did not want to go into the cage.

Hannah felt as droopy as Surprise's

tail. She didn't want him to go into the
cage either.

"Come on, boy," Juan coaxed. "Nobody's
going to hurt you." He opened the door of
the run.

Surprise stopped.

Juan tugged gently at his collar.

Surprise stuck his front legs out straight and wouldn't move.

Hannah's eyes filled up with tears. She could hardly see as she walked into the cage and squatted down in front of the kennel.

"Come on, Surprise," she said, and Surprise walked in.

8

Logan went through all the boxes till he found some paper and colored markers. He drew sign after sign.

Their phone wasn't connected yet, so he put his mom's cell phone number on the bottom.

He wished he could start putting the

posters up on every street corner, but there was no point—it was impossible for Bear to be anywhere around here. Logan would have to wait till tomorrow to go back to the beach.

Hannah and Surprise sat together in front of the kennel and looked around at the other dogs in their runs and kennels.

"With a bit of luck, his owner will find him quickly," said Juan.

Hannah nodded. For the first time, she really did hope that Surprise's family would find him.

"He seems like a friendly fellow—if the vet's happy with him, he might let him share a run with another dog."

Hannah thought Surprise would like that, but not as much as he'd like having his own home.

"And of course he can have a turn in the playground—that's the best part of a volunteer's job." Juan pointed to the dusty lawn in the middle of the U of kennels. "We let them out in here to run around, sniff all the new smells, play ball."

"Do you like playing ball?" Hannah whispered to Surprise, rubbing her tears dry against his shaggy shoulder.

Surprise pricked up his ears.

Juan laughed. "Okay! As soon as the vet says so, we'll have a game. But you have to be nice to an old man. I'm thinking you've got more energy than me!"

Hannah's ponytail swished. "I've got lots of energy," she said. "I could come and play with him. And clean his cage and feed him—and *everything*!"

"We'll have to ask your mom and dad," said Juan.

Hannah's mom and dad were still talking to Mona at the front desk.

"Hola, amigo!" squawked Gulliver.

"I've got an idea," said Hannah.

"So do we," said her mom.

Hannah felt a little candle of hope—they were going to let her keep Surprise until his real family found him!

"You know that this dog has to go back to his owners."

But if they don't want him . . . Hannah thought.

"And you know that our fence isn't tall enough to keep him in."

"I'll help you build a bigger one!"

Her dad smiled. "Our fence will work just fine."

"Come and see," said Mom, and Mona led them into the room with small animals in cages.

In the corner was a hutch with a fat black guinea pig.

9

Hannah liked guinea pigs, and this one was very cute. She picked him up. He was warm and soft. She thought about how happy she'd have been if she'd met this guinea pig this morning, before she'd met Surprise.

She wished she didn't feel like someone

at a party who'd got a carrot stick when everyone else had cake.

"Thank you," she said.

Mona was watching her carefully. "A guinea pig may be small," she said, "but he deserves to be wanted and loved. If you don't feel you can do that, you shouldn't take him."

Hannah hesitated. The little guinea pig wiggled warmly against her shoulder. "I'll love him," she said, and thought for a moment about how she would feed him and clean his hutch, play with him, and take him out to eat fresh grass every single day. "But I still need to tell you my idea: I want to be a volunteer like Juan."

"You're not really old enough," said Mona.

"But I could help him," said Hannah.

"I'm pretty old," Juan agreed. "Mix our ages up together and we'll both come out just right."

"You'll get upset when the owner comes to pick up this dog," said Mom.

"No, I won't!" said Hannah, but she knew that wasn't true.

"Only three days till school starts," said her mom. "You won't have time to look after this guinea pig properly and come to the shelter."

"The guinea pig or the shelter," said Dad. "Not both."

"Go home and think about it," said Mona.

That night, Logan squeezed between the boxes and sat on his bedroom floor to talk to his dad.

"Bear's a smart dog," his dad said. "He'll be heading back to the farm. We just have to figure out where he's got to and start searching there."

"He must feel so scared."

"That's why we have to keep searching. And hoping."

10

In Logan's nightmares, sometimes it was Bear that was lost, sometimes it was himself, and once his dad—but waking up was the worst of all because it was real.

It was very early, but his crammed-full room was too empty to stay in any longer. He crept quietly through the boxes to the kitchen. His mom was already dressed and studying a map as she drank her coffee.

"I've talked to Dad," she said, pointing to the map. "He's on his way here, fifteen miles from where Bear jumped out. He'll search from there toward the farm, and we'll search from there back to the beach."

Logan choked down a bowl of cereal, and they left.

In Hannah's dreams, her dad came home with a guinea pig in the back of his truck, and she kept hiding lost dogs in her bedroom—big and little, black, brown, white, and spotted, barking, bouncing dogs—till her room was so full she could hardly shut the door.

Hannah couldn't decide if it was a dream or a nightmare, but now that she was awake she was too happy to care. Her ponytail bounced as she skipped out to the kitchen.

"What have you decided?" asked her mom.

Hannah told her. She choked down a bowl of cereal, and when it was finally nine o'clock, they left.

Mona wasn't at the desk when they got to the Rainbow Street Shelter, but the gray parrot Gulliver was. "Can I help you?" he asked.

Hannah and her mom laughed, and Mona came in from the Small Animal Room. "So . . . are you here for the guinea pig?"

Hannah shook her head. "He's a very nice guinea pig," she said sadly, feeling as mean as if she'd left her best friend out of a secret.

"He is. But you can't take an animal home just because he's nice. You have to know he's the one for you."

"Hola, amigo!" squawked Gulliver as Juan came in.

"Hola," he said to the bird and smiled at Hannah. "Let's get going, helper!"

Hannah's ponytail bounced. She skipped behind him out to the kennels and across to Surprise.

The dog was standing at the front of his run. His head lifted when he saw Hannah and Juan, and his floppy white ear quivered.

"The vet checked him this morning," Juan said. "He's good and healthy, just feeling a bit lost."

"Poor lost Surprise," said Hannah. She knew his family must feel lost without him too. "I hope your family comes soon."

"We need to give him some breakfast," said Juan. "Then we'll clean out his run and give him a race around the playground."

He measured out a scoop of dog kibble

from a big bin. "Sit!" he told Surprise, and the dog sat while Hannah poured the kibble into his dish.

"Leave him alone while he eats, and we'll feed the others."

The kennel beside Surprise had been empty the day before, but there was a new dog in it now: a scruffy, shaggy little dog who would have been white if she hadn't been so dirty. She was lying down inside her kennel, her nose outside, watching.

"Don't go in," Juan warned. "Have a look from here."

Hannah squatted down outside the run. Behind the little dog's front legs she could see what looked like a row of fat, squirmy hot dog buns snuggled up to drink from their mother.

"Puppies!" Hannah breathed.

"Five of them," Juan said. "Dumped at the gate last night. Just a week old, so unless someone wants to take the mother and all the puppies, they'll have to wait another seven weeks to go to new homes."

Very quietly, he took a bowl of breakfast into the run and put it in front of the little dog. "She's scared, and she wants to protect her babies from us," he said. "She'll bite if she thinks she has to."

Juan fed the other dogs, and then let Hannah give a licky black Labrador his kibble. The Labrador was named Sam, and the sign on his cage said READY TO ADOPT.

"Now your pal can have a turn in the playground while I hose out his run." Juan clipped a leash onto Surprise's collar and handed it to Hannah.

Hannah shook her head.

"I'll hose," she said. It didn't seem fair to come to help and only do the fun things.

So she hosed the run clean, and then

Juan gave her the leash. Hannah and Surprise ran up and down and all around the playground.

"Come!" Juan called, and when they jogged over to him, he gave Surprise a little piece of dog biscuit.

"Good dog!" said Hannah, because Surprise had gone to Juan all by himself, even though she'd been at the end of the leash too.

Juan unclipped it. He showed Surprise a red ball. "Fetch!" he said and threw it hard across the playground.

Surprise shot after it so fast he caught it before it bounced, then dropped it at their feet. Hannah threw it over and over, and Surprise leaped and bounded from one side of the playground to the other, catching the ball till it was so slippery with slobber Hannah had to wipe it on the grass before she could throw it.

"Hannah!" called her mom. "Time to go home."

Hannah hugged Surprise tight and led him back to his run.

"What about the other dogs?" she asked, as she followed Juan out the gate.

"They'll get their turns. But your pal's the youngest. He takes the most running."

Logan and his mom put posters up on street corners for blocks in every direction from the Terri's Take Out. They walked far down the beach where people had seen Bear the day before. They drove around the streets where Bear might have run when he left the beach. They stopped to ask people walking their own dogs.

They never saw Bear, and no one they asked had seen him either.

They phoned all the vets and went to an animal shelter full of sad lost dogs, but none of them was Bear.

Logan's dad did all the same things, going back toward the farm, but he hadn't found Bear either. "We'll find him," he said again. "Don't give up hope."

"Just before Bear ran away," Logan whispered, hunkering down in his hidey-hole between the bedroom boxes, "I told him maybe he should have gone to live with you."

"Bear wasn't trying to run away," his dad said firmly. "He knows you love him, even if you said something you didn't mean. I'm guessing he jumped out that window to follow you, just got himself scared in the parking lot, took off, and got lost. Wherever he is right now, he'll be wanting to get back to you."

Logan tried to believe it, all through the next long day of looking and not finding, but it was getting harder to hope.

The day after that was going to be even worse.

It was the first day of school.

11

Logan's new school was about a hundred and eighty-five times bigger than his old one. He felt as lost as Bear just following the office lady down the halls to his classroom. He wondered if he'd ever find his way to the front gate again.

But wandering around the halls would have been better than sitting in a class waiting for his turn to stand up and say who he was and the most exciting thing he'd done this summer. *Hi, I'm Logan, and what I did this summer was lose my dog.*

Another boy, then a girl, then it would be his turn. The boy had just moved here too. He looked okay.

The girl stood up.

"I'm Hannah, and the most exciting thing that happened to me this summer was last Friday my dad came home with a dog in the back of his truck. It must have jumped in but he doesn't know where. It's got shaggy black fur, a white neck, three white paws, and a really cute floppy white ear. I call him Surprise, but—"

Logan jumped to his feet so fast his desk
tipped over. He didn't even notice.

"His name is Bear!"

"Logan!" exclaimed the teacher.

"Sorry," said Logan, picking his desk up. "But I lost my dog on Friday—and I think Hannah found him!"

The teacher decided that a lost-and-found dog was so exciting they should sort it out right then. Logan jumped to his feet again.

"Sit down, Logan," the teacher said. "You can't race off to the shelter in the middle of class. What you can do is make sure all the facts add up."

So they checked back and forth: "And his floppy ear pricks up when he's listening—"

"And he loves to play ball!"

"But his name was on his tag!"

"We'd never heard of a dog named Bear. We thought it was your last name!"

The only thing they couldn't explain was how Bear had got into Hannah's dad's truck, because the Terri's Take Out where Logan had lost him wasn't anywhere near where Hannah's dad had been working.

And they still had to wait till after school to be absolutely one-hundred-percent sure that it was really Bear waiting in the Rainbow Street Shelter.

Their moms were waiting at the gate.

"This is the girl who found Bear!" Logan shouted.

"This is the boy who lost Surprise!" shouted Hannah.

"We'll go straight to the shelter," said Logan's mom.

"And we'll show you the way there," said Hannah's mom.

Logan and his mom followed the other car through the streets toward the outskirts of town. They turned at the sign that said RAINBOW STREET SHELTER and parked at the end, by the old house with the rainbow painted on the front and a three-legged goat grazing in the yard.

Logan could hardly breathe as they walked up the path. His hands were shaking as he opened the door. His mom put her hand on his shoulder, but when she spoke to Mona her voice was shaky too.

"We think our dog is here."

Hannah and her mom stood at the shelter's back door and watched Logan and his mom cross to Surprise's run. But the dog wasn't Surprise anymore. He was Bear, and when he saw Logan, he began to yip and howl as if he was telling him all about the terrible time he'd had.

Mona opened the gate. Bear threw himself against Logan, and Logan threw himself down to hug Bear as if they would never let each other go again.

Hannah felt like she shouldn't be watching. She went back inside. Her mind was

happy because the dog's story had ended the very best way it could, but her eyes felt like crying.

"You could still change your mind about the guinea pig," her mom said gently.

Hannah thought about the old Labrador Sam and the frightened little dog with the five puppies and all the other dogs and cats that still needed to be comforted and played with while they waited for their owners or their new homes. She shook her head.

"I'll keep on coming," she said.

"We'd better phone your dad," Logan's mom said, but her phone rang before she had time to open it. She listened for a moment and smiled. "I think Logan would like to talk to you himself," she said, handing the phone over.

"I've just talked to someone who was at a gas station on Friday night. It sounds like the one where you lost Bear," said his dad's deep voice. "He saw a Border collie jump into the back of a pickup."

"It was my friend's dad's truck," said Logan.

Logan, his mom, and Bear walked back to the office. Hannah and her mom were still talking to Mona.

"Actually," Mona was saying, "the guinea pig went to a new home yesterday. But if you're sure you still want to do it, there are other dogs and cats who need the kind of help you gave Bear."

"Can I help too?" asked Logan.

"We don't normally allow children . . ." Mona began.

"Hola, amigo!" shrieked Gulliver when Juan walked in.

"I give up," said Mona. "As long as you do exactly what Juan says, you can come help too."

That night, curled up snug on his bedroom floor with Bear, Logan talked to his dad again.

"Give him a hug for me," said his dad. He sounded as if he had something stuck in his throat. "And one for you."

"One for you too," Logan said. His voice

sounded as if he had something stuck in his throat too. He wiped his eyes with his sleeve.

Bear licked the phone.

Logan hugged him hard, just like his dad had asked.

12

Every Saturday morning and on Tuesdays and Thursdays after school, Hannah and Logan went to the Rainbow Street Shelter. Their moms took turns driving, and after the first week, they stayed to help too. Logan's mom said that every time she helped another lost animal it was a thank-you for finding Bear.

At first Hannah's mom only wanted to help in the office or wash things in the kitchen, but she always came out to see the dog that Hannah was feeding or playing with.

The old black Labrador Sam left to live with a woman whose house was near the beach.

"But I have another job for you," said Juan. "Those puppies will be old enough to go to new homes in a couple of weeks. We could start getting them used to kids."

Hannah sat quietly in the run with the puppies. The mother dog watched her suspiciously, but finally decided that Hannah was not a danger, and even let her pat and pick up one fat squirmy puppy. He had a brown bottom, brown shoulders, and a white middle. "You look like a peanut!" Hannah whispered into his floppy white ear.

The next time she went, Juan and the mother dog let her take the puppies out to the playground. She rolled on the ground with the puppies tumbling around her, but when the peanut puppy licked her face she sat up under a tree and cuddled him against her. The puppy wriggled and licked her face with its rough tongue and milky breath; it scrambled over her legs and chewed on her finger with needle-sharp teeth. Hannah felt a warm bubble of love swell up inside her, and she rolled the puppy on his back, tickling his fat tummy and laughing so the swirling feelings didn't spill out in tears.

Logan was playing a tug-of-war with a bouncy beagle. He waved, and the beagle yanked the toy out of his hand, so that Logan tumbled over backward, the beagle bouncing proudly around him with the toy in his mouth.

A sharp knife of jealousy twisted through Hannah's shiny bubble because when Logan had cheered up the beagle, he'd go home to Bear. But Hannah had to leave this puppy here.

She bent low over the puppy to hide her face, and the puppy caught her drooping ponytail. Hannah laughed, picked him up again—and saw something she'd never imagined could happen.

Her mother was in the run, squatting down to talk to the nervous little mother dog, patting and soothing her while Juan cleaned out the puppies' wet newspapers. Hannah was so surprised she nearly dropped the puppy.

Hannah and her mother were both very quiet in the car on the way home. Logan thought he knew why. He'd seen Hannah's face when she held the puppy, and even though he knew there'd never be another dog as special as Bear, he knew that Hannah could love that puppy just as much as he loved Bear.

"Do you want to come in and say hello to Bear?" he asked when they dropped him off at his house.

Hannah shook her head no, and her ponytail drooped flatly down her neck.

That night, Hannah heard her parents talking after she'd gone to bed. She couldn't hear what they were saying but it sounded serious. She thought about how Logan and his mom had moved down here while his dad moved somewhere else, and all of a sudden she didn't feel jealous anymore. "If nothing bad happens and we don't have to move," she told herself, "I'll never complain again about not having a dog."

The next day after school, Hannah's mom called her out to the front yard when her dad got home. "Ready to go?" asked her dad.

"Where?" asked Hannah.

"Wait and see," said her dad, but he was grinning, and her mom was too, and Hannah knew everything was all right.

They drove down the familiar roads and turned at Rainbow Street. "But it's Friday!" said Hannah.

Her dad laughed and stopped the car. He laughed again when they walked into the shelter and Gulliver screeched "Hola, amigo!" But Hannah didn't laugh. All of a sudden Hannah was hoping so badly she could hardly breathe, and she was trying not to hope it because she was sure she could never breathe again if it didn't come true this time.

Juan and Mona met them. They looked serious, but Juan winked at Hannah, and the bubble of hope swelled a bit more. They all walked out to the dog runs, straight across to the scruffy little mother dog and her puppies.

"Our fence isn't tall enough for a big dog like Bear," said Hannah's dad. "But it would be fine for a dog with shorter legs."

"And the puppies aren't quite ready to go yet," said Juan. "There's time to fix up anything that needs fixing."

Now Hannah couldn't speak or breathe. Her mother squeezed her hand. "If you can come here to help these dogs, even though you thought they'd never be yours, we know you'll look after one of your own."

"Is this the little guy?" Juan asked, scooping up the brown and white puppy and putting him in Hannah's arms.

"The only thing is . . ." said Hannah's mom ". . . it probably won't be hard for the puppies to find good homes."

Juan nodded.

Hannah held the puppy tighter.

"So what about the mother?" asked Hannah's mom.

"That'll be harder," said Mona. "She's not a very pretty dog."

"She is so!" protested Hannah's mom. "I was just worrying about how lonely she'll feel when all her puppies leave."

"You think I should take the mother dog instead?" asked Hannah, and she knew she should feel happy to have any dog, but she belonged to this peanut puppy now and there was nothing she could do about it. The puppy squirmed closer to her face as if he thought so too.

"Of course not!" said her dad.

"Especially if the puppy's got anything
to say about it."

"The mother dog's for me," said
Hannah's mom.

13

What Bear liked best, almost more than anything else in the world, was riding in the back of the pickup truck when he and Logan stayed with Logan's dad.

The other thing he liked best, almost more than anything else in the world, was racing along the beach with Logan, sniffing the wind and barking at the waves.

But what he liked best of all, more than anything else in all the world, was Logan—because Logan was his boy.

What Peanut liked best, almost more than anything else in the world, was riding in the back seat of the car with his shaggy white mother and barking at the dogs in other cars.

The other thing he liked best, almost more than anything else in the world, was racing along the beach with Hannah, sniffing the wind and barking at the waves.

But what he liked best of all, more than anything else in all the world, was Hannah—because Hannah was his girl.

COMING SOON:

Turn the page for a sneak peek!

CAT SAVES OWNER'S LIFE!

Eighteen months ago, Mr. Edgar Larsen rescued a cat from the Rainbow Street Animal Shelter.

Last night, the cat returned the favor by rescuing his elderly owner.

Mr. Larsen, aged 89, fell in his kitchen, breaking his hip and losing consciousness.

Our reporters interviewed Mr. Larsen from his hospital bed. "Buster wasn't going to let me die," Mr. Larsen said. "He licked my nose and yowled in my ears till I woke up enough to call 9-1-1. That cat is a hero!"

However, in a sad twist to the tale, when Mr. Larsen's son arrived from New York City, the cat was missing. He is described as a large orange tabby cat. Anyone seeing him is asked to phone the Rainbow Street Animal Shelter.

From *Missing! A Cat Called Buster*